Elen's Island

Eloise: For Rosie M, Jo and Mum. I love you three more than all the sparkles in the sea.

Gabby: With all my love to Dave, for holding the fort and the babies.

Eloise Williams grew up in Llantrisant. She now lives in Saundersfoot, Pembrokeshire, very close to the beach where she walks her dog Watson Jones and collects sea glass. She worked in the theatre in wardrobe, then studied Drama. After working for over ten years as an actress, she studied for a Masters in Creative Writing at Swansea University.

Gabby Grant was born in Liverpool. After studying Illustration at Westminster University, she got a job making props for film and TV. She has illustrated four picture books, theatre posters and publicity material. She now juggles children's illustration, a little bit of prop-making and the bringing-up of three boys.

Author note
Huge thanks go to my editor, Janet, for being gracious, funny, kind and an absolute wizard with words.

To my dad for teaching me humour and the power of the ad-lib.

To Watson (dog) for not eating the paper this was written on.

Guy for being everything and for putting up with me.

Elen's Island

Eloise Williams

illustrated by

Gabby Grant

Firefly

First published in 2015
by Firefly Press
25 Gabalfa Road, Llandaff North, Cardiff, CF14 2JJ
www.fireflypress.co.uk
This edition 2017

Text copyright Eloise Williams 2015
Illustrations copyright Gabby Grant 2015
'Gran's map' illustration copyright Guy Manning 2015

A CIP catalogue record of this book is available from the British Library.

3 5 7 9 8 6 4 2

ISBN 9781910080207
ebook ISBN 9781910080214

This book has been published with the support of the Welsh Books Council.

Typeset by Elaine Sharples

Printed and bound by CPI Group (UK) Ltd, Croydon, CR0 4YY

Contents

Chapter One

The Journey

Elen's parents were completely hateful and horrible, disgusting and despicable, totally selfish and nasty and complete pig-heads, who weren't even as pretty as pigs. Elen screwed up her face hard. Tears stung her eyes but she wasn't going to let them fall. She felt like a kettle getting hotter and hotter and about to boil over.

How could they go on holiday without her?

She kicked her foot against the side of the train carriage, under the table.

How dare they send her off to stay with her stupid old grandmother, who she couldn't even remember meeting.

Elen pictured her grandmother, going by her sharp voice on the phone. A witch, slathered in black shawls, with a moustache like a caterpillar crawling across her top lip. She wouldn't have games consoles or anything interesting to do. Elen would probably be expected to spend her summer

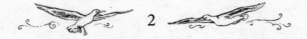

2

collecting stamps or making jam or the other junk that old people thought was interesting but was actually entirely boring and pointless.

Elen imagined her parents floating on blow-up beds in the Caribbean Sea. They sipped colourful cocktails, while the sun shone so brightly that they had to shade their eyes, and the sea was a glittering blue.

Outside the train window in Wales the sky was slate grey, with rain slashing across it in fat lines.

Elen kicked the wall again and tugged at her too-short fringe. Her mother had cut it so that it wouldn't need to be done for the rest of the summer. She glanced at her reflection and saw Frankenstein's monster glaring back at her.

The horrid woman who was escorting Elen to her grandmother offered her a sweet. Elen turned away to hide the huge hot tear rolling down her cheek. It bounced from her chin,

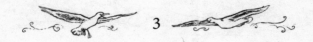

landed on her sleeve with a plop, and left the shape of a star in the material.

She'd show them. She would never speak to another grown-up ever again. Not her stupid parents, not her old moustache-lipped grandmother, not the horrid woman next to her who had noticed she was crying and was handing her a tissue.

Elen snatched the tissue without saying thank you. She felt proud of her bad manners. She was going to hold onto this nastiness, even though it made her feel like crying more.

Huge dark castles loomed out of the distant hills like giants. Sheep dotted the fields, munching miserably on grass. She kept having to wipe condensation off the window to see out. Every time Elen wiped it, she caught another glimpse of Frankenstein's monster.

It was cold. It was wet. It was awful.

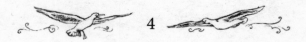

Even the rattle and tug of the train was against her:

'*Ne-ver, ne-ver,*
you are ne-ver going back,
never going back!' it said over and over.

'You'll have a wonderful time.' The woman in black tried again. 'I grew up there. We had some fun! I remember once there was a whole beach full of seals. Can you imagine it? The whole surface of the sand seemed to be moving.' She smiled. 'You'll love the water. It's so clear and clean and there are forests of seaweed in it. You never get seaweed like it anywhere else.'

She could certainly go on, Elen thought.

'Oh and the birds! There are these black and white ones with long red beaks called oystercatchers. They sound like squabbling teenagers when they get going. *Peep-peep-peep*, they go. *Peep-peep-peep*.'

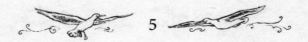

Elen looked around the carriage to make sure no one she knew could see her listening to this woman's bird impressions.

'And seagulls, the baby ones, make a sound like a kitten: *mew-mew-mew*. I saw one take a sausage roll out of a toddler's hand once. Swallowed it whole!'

On, and on, and on.

'When we were kids we used to explore the caves and dig for pirate treasure. We'd jump off Smugglers' Rocks into the sea and the fish would swim around us. Once I turned round and there was a jellyfish the size of a dustbin lid right next to me!'

Elen was a bit interested in monster jellyfish, but managed to disguise it by plugging in her earphones and pretending to be engrossed in the music. She closed her eyes and tried not to think about her mum and dad.

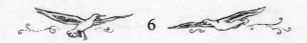

Because she was trying not to think about them they were, of course, the only thing she could think of.

'I want to come with you!' she had screamed.

'I've already told you it's not that kind of holiday.' Her father looked at his watch.

'I don't care what kind of holiday it is. I want to come.' It flashed through her mind that they might like it so much abroad they would never come back.

'Daddy's right, Elen. You'll have your holiday and we'll have ours.' They smiled at each other weakly and her dad put his arm around her mum's shoulders.

Elen couldn't believe they could smile when she felt so left out.

She picked up one of her mother's best vases and threw it, flowers and all, across the living

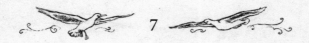

room. Bright orange petals scattered on the carpet.

This didn't make them change their minds.

Elen came home from school to find the woman in black waiting for her with a suitcase in one hand and a goodbye letter from her parents in the other. They'd signed it: 'See you soon. Love Mummy and Daddy.' Elen crumpled it into a ball and threw it in the bin. The woman in black looked sad then told Elen what her name was. It was a stupid name which Elen forgot immediately.

The train jolted and brought her back from her thoughts.

She glanced slyly at the woman in black. She had given up trying to convince Elen of the brilliance of seaweed, and had also put her earphones into her ears.

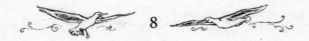

8

Another grown-up had given up on her.

Her fringe scratched against her forehead. Another tear slipped down her cheek. She rubbed at her face, scolding herself for acting like a little kid, and tried to pull herself together. She had to be brave, Elen told herself. She might be going away on her own for the first time. She might be surrounded by lots of people she didn't know. She was definitely fed up and freezing and feeling like being sick all over herself. But she was smart and clever and nearly ten years old.

Elen tried not to shudder as she imagined the horrors that awaited her on the island.

Chapter Two

Aberglad

When they arrived at Aberglad, a wonderful thing happened. The sky began clearing from grey to the brightest, cleanest blue. A rainbow hovered above the town. Children chattered in the streets and strings of brightly coloured bunting flapped in the breeze. The sea was as sparkly as a crystal when they walked down to the harbour.

'It's always brighter in the west,' the woman said.

Elen remembered that the woman's name was Nerys, which seemed like a pretty name when she thought about it properly.

'That's where I grew up.' Nerys pointed to a tiny pink cottage. It was the size of a doll's house and had millions of flowers in its small garden. 'Winkle Cottage.'

'It's lovely,' Elen replied, startling Nerys.

Nerys smiled. Elen smiled shyly back at her. She felt a bit guilty but also quite proud of how long she'd managed to keep silent. It was the longest she'd not said anything since she'd learned to talk.

'It is lovely. Bit on the pokey side, mind you.' Nerys waved to someone in a passing car.

'I can see that,' Elen said, then worried that she'd picked the wrong time to joke, but Nerys

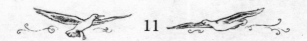

beamed down at her and laughed loudly. Elen laughed too. The storm had passed inside her as well as in the sky.

'Come on. Let's get a wriggle on or we'll miss the boat,' said Nerys. They hurried on to the harbour wall and reached some rickety stone steps.

Elen read the words 'Dead Man's Steps' on the sign at the top and, shocked, looked at Nerys. Nerys pointed at a door with a large skull and crossbones above it. 'That's where they used to put people who died from the plague so that they wouldn't have to step over their rotting bodies in the street. Imagine it. All the flies and the maggoty stench!'

'That's gross.' Elen was starting to like Nerys. No one talked to her like this usually. Everyone else treated her like a kid.

'If anyone died at sea and their body washed up without identification they would throw

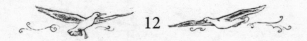

12

them in there too. There's an awful lot of sailors there. Some of them were buried with their treasure hoard. Or so people say. I doubt if it's true though.'

Elen stared at the door and felt the hairs on the back of her neck prickle.

'We should've left earlier,' Nerys panted, as they trotted down the steps. 'I'm running out of puff.'

'What happens if we miss the boat?' Elen asked, almost jogging to keep up.

'We can't miss the boat. It's the last one today and there might not be another one for a week if the weather forecast is right.' Nerys looked up grimly at the shiny sky. 'Now come on, slowcoach, or we'll have to swim for it.'

'Not with the size of those jellyfish, thanks very much.'

Little pastel-coloured houses surrounded the harbour walls and lots of people bustled about, shopping and fishing, gardening and chatting. Nerys greeted nearly all of them by name. A man shook a lobster at her. It looked as if the

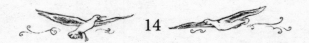

lobster knew Nerys as it waggled its claw in the air.

'You'll soon get to know everyone around here,' she told Elen. 'And they'll want to know everything about you!'

As if on cue, a woman stood in their way with a hen cuddled close to her chest. She had bright pink hair. Elen marvelled at how much she looked like a human candyfloss.

'Hello, Nerys love. Who's this, then?' She squinted at Elen.

'Sorry, Sally. Got to catch the last boat over. No time for a chat.'

Nerys tried to get past her. The candyfloss-on-legs persisted. 'Well, when you've got time, love, I want to tell you about my new collection of hens. Lovely things, hens. Lovely eggs they lay. Lovely. Lovely. I said to Mrs Williams only this morning...'

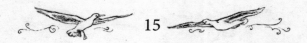

Nerys dragged Elen on with a look that said: 'I told you so'.

The tide was in and cheerful boats bobbed red and yellow against it, their bells *chinkle-tinkling* and their chains tugging against their anchors.

'We're going to have to run!' Nerys exclaimed.

And they did. Past the lobster pots and the old buoys with seaweed beards, past the children crabbing and the adults eating sarnies, and along the harbour wall, Nerys waving her hands to get the attention of a man untying a boat which looked a little the worse for wear.

'Mr Evans!' Nerys shouted.

He looked up and waved back, handing the rope to a boy. Elen and Nerys clattered up to them.

'Hello, Nerys. Long time no see.' The man smiled.

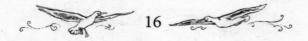

'I've … been … working … away … Mr Evans,' Nerys told him between breaths.

'Ah, all the young ones go off and they very rarely come back.' He shook his head. 'Who is this then?'

'This is Elen, Mr Evans. She's staying with her grandmother on the island.' Nerys pushed Elen forwards.

Elen held out her hand to Mr Evans. 'Very pleased to meet you, sir.'

Mr Evans threw his head back and laughed. The boy laughed slyly too.

'Very polite we are.' Mr Evans chortled. 'But you can call me Captain Evans and I'll call you Able Seaman Elen.'

Elen would rather he just called her Elen but she knew it would be rude to say so.

He looked as much like a sea captain as it was possible to look in his yellow wellies and

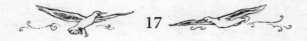

Sou'wester hat. His curly white beard was so fluffy Elen wanted to give it a tug to see if it was real. As she stared at his beard, he started to scratch it.

'So Mrs Thomas is your granny then, eh?'

'Elen has never met her,' Nerys said.

'I have, but when I was a baby so I can't really remember her,' Elen added.

Mr Evans winked at the boy, who had now finished untying the boat. 'That old boot! Oh you poor little thing. You'll be lucky to get any sense out of her. She hasn't spoken to me in nigh on twenty years!'

Perhaps he had done something to make her cross. Elen wondered if maybe she wasn't the only one in her family who sulked.

His face changed from joyful to stern in five seconds flat. 'Seriously, you be careful with her. She's a strange one.' He looked straight into

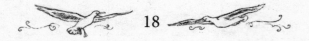

Elen's eyes. She could tell he wasn't joking. She felt a shiver run down her spine.

'OK. Well, take good care of her, won't you.' Nerys patted Elen on the head and passed her luggage to Mr Evans. Mr Evans gave it to the boy, who threw it roughly down from the top of the steps, almost breaking it. The boy stared spitefully at Elen as if daring her to complain.

'Aren't you coming with me?' If she hadn't already cried all the way here, and if the boy wasn't now looking at her as if she was a complete baby, Elen could easily have started bawling again.

'I've got to go and see my own family now, lovely,' Nerys said. 'But I'll come over in a week or so and check you are all right.'

Elen looked down at her feet and started a brand new silent sulk. Nerys leaned over and hugged her awkwardly.

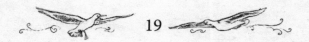

'All aboard!' Mr Evans shouted, ushering Elen into the boat. It rocked violently as it was released from the quay and Elen almost lost her footing.

The boy laughed. 'We've got ourselves a right landlubber here, Captain Evans.'

'She'll soon get the weight of the water,' Mr Evans called back.

The boy sneered at Elen. She walked confidently to the seat so that he could see she was actually fantastic at being in a boat.

She could feel her tummy rolling over, though she wasn't sure if it was the motion of the boat or fear of what was waiting for her on the island. The wooden bench was wet with sea spray and soaked through her trousers immediately. The whole thing reeked of fish.

Elen stared at the deck as the boat chugged out of the harbour into the open water. She could feel the boy's sullen glare burning holes into her back and could hear Nerys shouting goodbye but she didn't turn to wave. Nerys had been employed by her parents to deliver her like a package and that was exactly what she had done. As soon as Elen's foot had hit the deck of the boat, she'd finished her job.

Elen was alone in a boat that stank of fish. Totally, completely and stinkily alone.

Chapter Three

Gran's shack

It was two miles to the island. The sun started to drop from the sky at an amazing speed.

The sun sets in the west, Elen knew that, but she'd never thought it would sink so quickly. She almost forgot to be angry as she watched it. The colours of the sunset made it look as if the sun was burning the water. The boat sent water rubies and amber spray high into the air as it bounced against the waves.

Mr Evans, standing at the helm, pointed to the right. She turned and saw dolphins breaking the surface with their fins. Elen had seen a dolphin before in a zoo. It was very different to see them in the wild like this. Her heart almost leapt out of her chest as one of the dolphins broke the surface and seemed to fly through the air. It was all she could do not to yell with sudden happiness.

'Bottlenose dolphins, Able Seaman Elen,' he

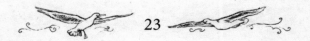

called, his beard alive in the wind like wriggling worms.

Elen guessed he wanted her to reply, 'Aye, aye Captain.' Or something equally childish. She nodded curtly and sat on her hands.

The sky turned from fiery red to burnt orange, to cerise pink, to indigo and eventually to violet. The island loomed up ahead of them, purple and monstrous in the growing darkness. She wasn't going to be scared.

'There she is, Able Seaman Elen. Waiting at the dock. The old boot,' Mr Evans shouted. Elen looked. She could just make out an old woman bent over a stick, waiting. It was impossible to tell whether she was smiling or not from this distance. Her face was in shadow.

They pulled up alongside the jetty and Elen's luggage was thrown off. People here didn't care too much for expensive suitcases.

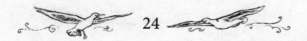

Elen climbed out of the boat gingerly. The motion of the waves was making her stomach roil.

The bent old woman stared at her suspiciously.

'Hello Gran. I'm Elen. Very pleased to meet you.' Elen wondered if she should curtsey or go for a firm handshake.

'Just like your mother.' The old woman raised her gnarled stick to point up a small lane, then turned and started hobbling along it.

'Nice to see you, Mrs Thomas!' Mr Evans called after her cheerily, if a little sarcastically. She made a 'GRRRR' noise at him, then carried on up the road.

I'll carry my own bags then, shall I? Elen thought. Perhaps she couldn't expect a woman with a walking stick to carry luggage for her and anyway she'd have to get used to doing things for herself here. She struggled to trundle her

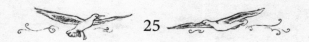

suitcase on wheels along the dark lane as it got narrower and more and more creepy.

At the end of the road was a shack so dark and unwelcoming, so dirty and scary, that Elen couldn't begin to imagine who could live in it.

Gran pushed open the front door and walked in.

Elen stood outside and for a moment wondered if she could make herself a home out of sand on the beach, but then she took a deep breath and went in.

Inside, she wished she'd taken an even deeper breath, because the smell made it hard to breathe at all. A mix of mushy peas and ham with a bit of dog breath and cheesy sock thrown in. Elen fought the urge to make a disgusted noise. She followed her grandmother through to the kitchen. Candles lit the table and threw long dancing shadows against the walls.

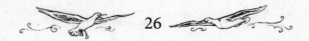

'I expect you'll be hungry if you are anything like your mother,' Gran said.

Elen took umbrage at this comment. Her mother may have gone off on holiday without her, but she was still her mother.

'I am very much like my mother, but I am not hungry,' she stated firmly, quaking in her shoes a little.

'Of course you are hungry. Young people always are. They just forget about it because they are too busy doing things. Always up to something. Sit down.'

Elen looked at the pot on the kitchen hob which was bubbling and hissing with a loud *flubble-ssssstttt-ping* sound every few seconds.

She sat at the far side of the table as the old woman walked towards the pot with a ladle.

'Do you want one scoop or two?'

Elen didn't want to be rude but she didn't

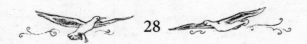

think there was any way she could eat anything that smelled like that.

'I think I'm probably allergic to it,' she lied, feeling bad but silently promising to do something good in the future to make up for it.

Gran guffawed loudly. 'Your face! You don't think I'd actually make you eat this, do you!'

Elen laughed too. Maybe her grandmother wasn't all that strange. She had a sense of humour at least.

'What is it?' Elen asked, glad to have something funny to talk about.

'Liquid magic.' Her grandmother's face shone with joy and the steam spiralling up from the pot. 'There are strange things on this island. Plants and animals so beautiful you wouldn't find them anywhere else. We've had mermaids spotted off our shores and you can hear pirate ghosts digging for the treasure that they've

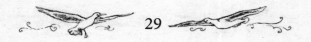

buried years ago. Anything can happen here. Anything at all.'

It was difficult for Elen not to feel the excitement her grandmother felt for this place, but she just about managed it.

'Of course you'll just think I'm a lonely old woman spouting a complete load of claptrap!' Gran guffawed again, then returned to stirring her spell.

Elen looked around. A box in the centre of the table caught her eye. It was carved with pictures of fairies in mid-flight and deer and rabbits. Its clasp was ornate and looked even older than her grandmother. There must be something very beautiful in it, Elen decided, her fingers creeping across the table.

'And you can keep your dirty paws off that!' Gran flew across the kitchen. She grabbed the box and grasped it tightly.

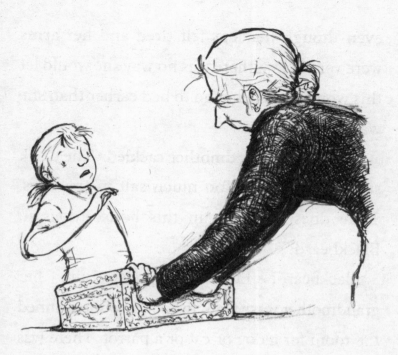

'That's enough for today. I've made you a cheese sandwich. Eat it and then go to bed,' she said, then hobbled out of the kitchen shaking her head. A hand-held oil lamp lit the stairs. 'Turn the lights off as you come. We like it dark here.'

'What time is it exactly?' Elen asked. Her bedtime was never this early, she was sure, and

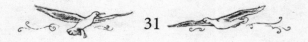

even though her legs felt tired and her arms were very heavy, there was no way she would let this woman make her go to bed earlier than she was allowed.

'Time?' her grandmother cackled. 'The clock stopped working. Too much salt in the cogs. Time doesn't matter in this house, does it, Blackbeard?'

Blackbeard? Elin was pretty sure her grandmother wasn't talking to her, so she scanned the room for a dog or cat or a parrot. There was none.

Elen had done a project on pirates in school and Blackbeard had been dead for a very long time. Gran talked to dead people. Perhaps there were dead people in this house. Perhaps there was the ghost of a pirate right behind her. Elen swung around.

To her relief, there was nothing there.

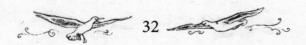

Her grandmother shouted, 'Just keep your nose out of my business and I'll keep my nose out of yours. I expect you'll find it boring here. Most young people do.'

Elen agreed. She decided she would eat her sandwich to keep her strength up in case she needed to swim back to the shore.

She could hear the crabbity old woman talking to herself upstairs then slamming a door. Elen put her cheese sandwich in her pocket and struggled past the salted clock and up the stairs with her wheelie suitcase, dreading what she would find at the top. There was only one door ajar. She peeked around it, then entered cautiously.

The room was lit by a small lamp and decorated in a deep blood red. Paintings of pirate galleons and famous pirates hung on the walls. A human skull balanced on a shelf just

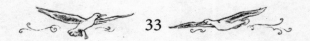

above the bed, with lots of books on pirate lore. It was odd but brilliant.

Elen took the skull down to examine it and plonked herself on the bed to eat her slightly squashed sandwich. She wasn't sure what to make of anything. Her grandmother certainly had interesting taste and perhaps some people would call her quirky. She wondered what she kept in that box that was so important and secret. It could be pirate treasure maps. It could be an antique pearl necklace or an opal tiara she was keeping all to herself so that she wouldn't have to give her family a share because she hated them so much.

Still feeling the ground shift and heave after her boat ride, Elen lay down on the quilt for a good hard think. She tugged at her fringe and fell fast asleep wondering about the contents of that box and how she was going to get her hands on it!

Chapter Four

The Island

Elen woke with the sun streaming onto her face through a gap in the curtains. She still had her travelling clothes on and her hair had tied itself into a tight knot around her bobble during the night. She checked her fringe to see if it had grown. It hadn't.

Tiptoeing around the room she listened for any noises. There were crows cawing from the trees outside and the echo of the waves, but she couldn't hear anything else. She got changed quickly and promised her reflection she would wash her face later.

Pulling the curtains apart, she looked out at the view. There, at the end of the lane, was the open sea glistering its forget-me-not blue beneath a cloudless sky. Tiny sailing boats bobbed on its surface like toys and Elen could clearly make out the happy little buildings of Aberglad. She showed the skull the view, then placed it on the window where it could look out. It might be her only friend here.

Her old life seemed a very long way away, but just as she was about to get upset again her stomach made a loud noise to tell her how hungry it was. This rumble was mixed with a strange, tickling feeling of excitement.

She crept across the landing and gently knocked on her grandmother's door. There was no reply. She knocked again a little more loudly.

If Gran was out she could take a sneaky peek in that box. She wouldn't steal it. She might just borrow it. Her hand shook as she reached for the handle.

The door was locked. Elen thought that if you locked a door in your own house you must be hiding something extremely valuable on the other side.

There was nothing else she could do, so she investigated the rest of the untidy house. She couldn't find anything particularly interesting about the other rooms except for a great deal of dusty paperwork and mess, so she went to the kitchen in search of food.

 38

At the centre of the kitchen table was a picnic and a hand-drawn map of the island. 'Go and explore if you can be bothered,' was written beneath it in a spidery *scrabbily* scrawl.

Elen examined the map. It was quite artistically done, she thought, though she doubted the sharks her grandmother had drawn in the sea actually existed.

Mr Evans had warned her on the way over that some parts of the island were treacherous and unsuitable for kids without a responsible adult. Elen decided that even though her grandmother was quite obviously being irresponsible, it would be naughty if she ignored her order to 'Go and explore'.

Elen was very good at reasoning things in her own favour. One day she planned to become a lawyer.

Seal Point

The Forest

The Lanterns

Sand Dunes

Strumble Sands

Smugglers' Rocks

Caves

Lighthouse

Blackbeard's Bay

dolphins

N

She poked her head out of the back door. Her mouth dropped open. The garden was absolutely the messiest thing she had ever seen. A rusty wheelbarrow filled with mud was turned on its side. A hose had wrapped its way around a tree, like a slithering snake. Upturned pots lay cracked and broken with jagged edges like fangs. All manner of rubbish had collected in the bushes and brambles and sharp thorns grew up every wall.

Elen walked around the outside of the house wondering why someone would want to live in such a sty. She didn't like tidying her bedroom at home, but she would never let it get this bad.

She stopped at the front door and wiped the mucky filth from a sign. It said 'The Lanterns'. There were some lanterns hanging above it which looked as if they were last lit in Victorian times, if ever. Elen imagined them filled with candles beaming happy warmth through

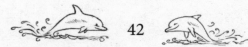

sparkling glass. Someone might have loved this house once upon a time.

The view was amazing. Looking at the beach at the end of the lane, she couldn't help the overwhelming urge to run. Her feet pounded down the path, which seemed much less creepy in daylight, scaring up butterflies from the grasses. They fluttered around her, yellow and white, orange and metallic blue. She kept running, past big purple flowers and daisies still curled into their pink edges in the shade. Past dunes golden with scratching sand. Past trees all bent in one direction from years of wind. She was out of puff but she kept on running across the peach-smooth beach, leaving the first footprints on the creamy surface.

Elen kicked off her shoes, plonked down her bag and ran straight into the water. She ran straight back out again. It was freezing!

43

Tentatively she put her toes back in. It was like putting them into an ice lolly at first, but as she got used to it the water seemed to warm. Elen imagined it was heating up just for her. Little pieces of seaweed drifted around her feet. A tiny fish darted towards her toe, then sensed danger and backed off.

Elen kept as still as she could and watched the life beneath the water's surface. A crab waddled past sideways not seeming to notice her at all. A purple jellyfish, cute and small, puff-balled its way towards her, reminding her of the giant jellyfish Nerys had talked about. Elen looked around anxiously for one, but then forgot it again.

People said the sea was blue but now she could see that wasn't correct. It was gold under the sun and silver at the tip of waves, light green close to her feet, royal blue on the horizon and pale blue closer in. There were

white horses where the current was choppy and sparkling sequins of light in patches. Elen wondered if she could do a painting of it for her mum.

Her mum. Elen felt sad again. Partly because her mum and dad had gone on holiday without her and partly because she felt bad she'd been so nasty to them. They seemed to have a lot of problems lately. They argued way into the night. They worked hard every day. Perhaps they deserved a holiday.

Elen looked at Aberglad across the water and wished that she could turn time back. To when she had thrown her mum's vase. She wondered again why her mum didn't speak to her grandmother much, but her grandmother wasn't easy to talk to, so perhaps her mum was right.

She sat down and studied her map. The pen and ink drawing must have taken a while to

complete. Her grandmother's house was clearly marked with an x (although it should really have been marked with a festering compost heap). The beach was called 'Strumble Sands'. Little dunes were drawn with a shaky hand and curly lines for the sea.

That meant that 'Seal Point' was to the west and 'Blackbeard's Bay' to the east at each end of the island. Elen was on the south side and 'Smugglers' Rocks' and the lighthouse were to the north. There was so much to explore.

The far end of the beach slid into the ocean and looked as if that might be where the world actually ended. Elen walked along the edge of the water looking at the patterns her feet were making in the sand. She ran in circles to confuse anybody following her. She hopped on one leg for as long as she could, then balanced on her tiptoes so that the print of her heel disappeared and it looked as if

some strange animal had been there. She whooped and hiccupped and *phizzled* with laughter.

'Sssssh!' An angry voice stopped her in her tracks.

Elen looked up to find the boy from the boat staring scornfully down at her from his perch on a rock.

He pointed at the water. 'You're scaring the fish away.'

'Oh, sorry.' Elen's voice came out more than a little nastily. She didn't like the boy's tone.

'What do you want anyway?' the boy asked.

'I don't want anything, thank you very much.' She resisted adding, 'Especially from you.'

'Then what are you doing on my island?'

Elen thought he had the most arrogant, obnoxious face she had ever seen.

'It's not your island. It doesn't belong to anybody. I've got just as much right to be here as you. My grandmother lives here.'

The boy laughed. 'Oh yes. That crazy lady is your grandmother. Well, that explains a lot.'

'She's not crazy,' Elen spat. 'She's brilliant.

She's the best grandmother anyone could wish for.'

Although this was a lie, there was no way she was going to allow this stupid boy to insult her family.

'What's that?' Elen had spotted something moving around in the upturned hat next to him.

'It's a puffin, obviously,' the boy said as if he was talking to an eight year old.

'What's a puffin?'

Elen thought it was a funny kind of word for a funny kind of animal. It was black and white with a bright red beak and strange, sad-looking eyes. It looked like a cross between a duck and a penguin.

'Looks like craziness runs in the family,' he said, reeling his line in and resting the puffin gently in the crook of his arm. 'I'm going to have to find something else for my dinner. Thanks very much.'

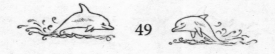

'Yeah, thanks very much to you as well,' Elen retorted, though it made no sense. It didn't really matter because the boy disappeared off the beach down an almost hidden path through the dunes.

What a stupid, idiotic, horrible boy, Elen thought. What an outrageously dull and irritating person. There was no way she could ever be friends with someone as ridiculously horrid as him.

She kicked at the sand and watched the flish-flash of the fish as they returned to safe waters. She wished that she was a fish, swimming merrily with its school of friends. Or perhaps their school was as difficult as her school was. The truth was that however horrible the boy had been, it would have been good to have made a new friend here, so far from home.

 50

Chapter Five

An Unexpected Meeting

The boy had put Elen in a terrible mood. She set off towards Blackbeard's Bay. Even though any pirate treasure would probably have been stolen or washed away years ago, perhaps she'd be lucky and find just one chest. Or an egg-sized sapphire so she could buy a house and live on her own forever.

She imagined doing whatever she wanted: staying up till all hours, watching as much television as possible, partying with all the friends she'd make when she was rich and important.

She imagined her parents begging at the gate of her mansion while she sat in her jacuzzi and ignored them. They wore rags and looked pathetic. But however hard she tried, when she imagined them, Elen couldn't shift the cocktails out of their hands or take off their sunglasses.

She stomped over the salt-grazed grasses, stamping them down hard. She was going to step on a pretty yellow flower, but changed her mind at the last second and twisted her ankle trying to avoid it. She limped on.

Elen didn't stop at the edge of the scary dark forest. She was too busy being cross to notice it. When her anger started to simmer down, she

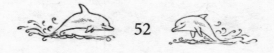

realised how dark it was. Shadows moved at the corner of her eyes. There was a heady pungent smell and all sorts of strange noises. Shrieks and whinnies and pops and squeals and screams and shudders and *blurps* were all around her.

The sky was a jigsaw of blue way, way above. She fumbled to look at the map, but her fingers shook and she had no idea which direction was where anymore.

She would not be afraid. She was almost ten years old. She was practically a grown-up. She tugged at her too-short fringe.

'Whoooooooooo.' Something flew past her head too close, clipping her ear.

Elen forgot about her twisted ankle and ran, stumbling over tree roots, sticks cracking beneath her feet, the circus of strange noises snapping at her heels. She was one of the fittest pupils in her class and could run very fast. She

 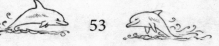

could run so fast that she sometimes found it hard to stop.

'Arrrgggghhhhhh!!!!!' She knocked into something and landed in a messy heap on the floor. Lying face down with pine cones digging into her ribs and a spiky twig up her nose, she held her breath and waited for the worst. She was too afraid to look up in case the thing she'd hit was some strange zombie dead person.

'What do you think you are doing?' the thing raged.

Elen cowered. She was sorry for being so nasty about her parents and wished she could apologise for all her horrible thoughts.

'You again. Are you following me? Of all the stupid things to do! Running straight into someone while they are trying to find berries,' the thing ranted.

As far as Elen knew, the terrible creatures in

scary stories ate children for dinner, not berries. She peered through her fingers.

The horrible boy stood in front of her.

Elen jumped to her feet. 'What do you mean, am I following you? If you hadn't been in the way I wouldn't have fallen over you. Anyway, you shouldn't pick berries in a forest. They can poison you.'

'Don't tell me what to do. Who do you think you are?' The boy's face started to look more like a beetroot than a boy. The puffin examined her quizzically from the boy's pocket.

'I'm Elen, thanks very much, and I know all about berries. We did a project on it in school. The ones you buy in the shop are OK but you need specialist knowledge to pick your own.' Elen drew herself up to her full height.

'I was looking for wild strawberries, which are perfectly safe, thanks. Anyway, I was named

after a berry so I should know all about them.'
The boy laughed at her. She thought perhaps she
should encourage this boy to eat something
poisonous.

Elen wondered what berry he was named
after. Not a blackberry or a raspberry because
they were too nice. She might call him a
gooseberry, because they were sour and bitter
and hairy and made you want to spit. She kicked
at the floor with temper, sending some bits of
fallen leaf towards the boy.

'Oy.' He kicked the floor back towards her. A
particularly sharp stick struck her leg and
scratched it hard. A trickle of blood ran down
into her sock.

There was a moment of complete silence.
Only the puffin dared to blink.

'GRRRRRRR!' Elen made the noise she'd
heard her grandmother make. Her leg stung

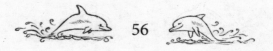

where the stick had scratched her. She turned and strode away.

'Hey. I'm sorry. I didn't mean to hurt you. Are you all right?' he called after her.

She carried on striding with even bigger steps.

'Where are you going?' he yelled.

Without turning around she shouted back in her most authoritative voice, 'Blackbeard's Bay. Not that it's any of your business.'

'Well, unless it's moved you won't find it that way. Come on, I'll show you.'

Elen weighed up her options. She could stay in the forest forever and die of starvation or from eating poisoned berries. Or she could follow the boy. She followed the boy, but she glared at him.

'Of course it is hard to find your way around if you aren't used to being on an island.' He smiled at her.

'What makes you think I'm not used to islands?' Elen spat out.

'It's kind of obvious.' The boy clearly knew his way as he led her through the foliage.

'Oh, and I suppose you know everything?' Elen crossed her arms as she walked. It was something her mum did when she was annoyed. When she realised that, Elen uncrossed her arms.

'Not everything, no, but I know my way around here like the back of my hand.' He showed her his hand as if it actually had a map printed on it. 'I've been coming here over and over since I was a kid, so if you need a guide then I'm your man.'

'Why on earth would someone want to come here over and over? It seems like a pretty dull place to me.'

The puffin stared at her. Elen wished she hadn't got off on the wrong foot with this boy,

even though it was completely his fault for being obnoxious and unfriendly. Perhaps he just didn't like people. He certainly didn't like her, which was a shame as she desperately wanted to ask him if she could have a hold of the puffin.

'Oh well, I'm sorry you think it's so boring, little miss know-it-all, but perhaps shipwrecks and caves aren't your thing at all. Perhaps the most spectacular storm in the world isn't something you'd like to see. Maybe you don't like watching lightning in sheets or waves as big as mountains.'

It was his turn to stride away.

Elen jogged to catch up with him.

'There are really waves as big as mountains?'

'Of course there are. You wouldn't believe how big they get, or the noise.' He put his hands over his ears and the puffin nodded at Elen as if in agreement.

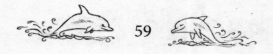

'Not tsunamis?'

'No, you idiot, they are just brilliantly massive waves and the wind screeches through your ears like a million banshees. That's how Captain Beaky here got hurt.' The boy held the puffin up for her to get a closer look. He really did have the most comical face. 'I found him after the last storm. His leg was all funny. I think it might have been broken. I'm not sure if something fell into his burrow or if he got hurt while he was walking about, but I found him lying on the floor so I've been looking after him till he's better.'

'He's beautiful.' Elen thought the puffin was one of the most magical animals she had ever seen.

'He was only a puffling then. He'll be all better soon and when he is I'll release him into the wild.' Elen could tell that the boy really loved

Captain Beaky. He went up in her estimation quite a lot after that.

'Come on, we need to get a move on. There's a storm coming!' He dashed ahead. Elen raced after him.

They were suddenly out into the light and overlooking a shimmering turquoise bay. The boy looked at the sky, shook his head and whistled.

'This storm is going to be absolutely terrifying, you lucky thing!' He patted Elen on the back. 'I've got to get off before it hits. That's my kayak down there.'

He pointed to a bright orange boat that had left a line in the sand where it had been dragged away from the tide's edge. 'I'll see you on the other side of the storm!'

Elen attempted a smile and glanced back at the forest in alarm.

'You don't have to go that way, don't worry! Just up to the lighthouse and then follow the straight road down. Easy.' He ran off towards the kayak then ran back.

'Rowan.' He put his hand out to Elen.

'Elen.' She grudgingly shook it.

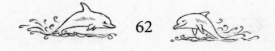

He ran off again, hugging Captain Beaky to him, and launched his boat into the flattest, calmest bay imaginable. Elen waited for him to disappear around the side of the cove and out of sight.

In the distance a roll of grey cloud appeared. The sound of the air changed. Even the gulls stopped their raucous cries. Elen wrinkled her nose. She thought about checking for scattered jewels in Blackbeard's Bay, but decided to be cautious and hurried towards the lighthouse. It was unlikely that a storm was coming, but she wasn't going to risk it.

She scurried up the higgledy-piggledy path and came face to face with her grandmother.

'Better get home. There's a storm coming,' Gran snarled, rising from a bench that had a brass plaque on it:

JACK – GONE FISHING.

'I know, everyone keeps saying that, but the sky is almost completely blue and...'

Elen was already talking to her grandmother's back. The old woman hurried off. Despite her walking stick, she was already quite far ahead.

How rude, Elen thought. Perhaps she wouldn't follow her. Perhaps she would stay out here by herself for as long as she wanted.

A humungous raindrop chose Elen's nose as its place to land. 'Plip.' Then another hit her elbow. 'Plap.' A third fell right on the crown of her head. 'Plop.'

She would stay in a strop with her grandmother, but perhaps it would be more effective if she stropped in the house near her rather than here alone on the cliff top, Elen reasoned.

Drops started pelting her as she sped up the rickety path. They splattered her as she ran

down the road towards The Lanterns. By the time she reached the front door the rain was lashing down and the unlit lanterns were creaking on their hinges in the wind.

Elen was soaked through and hungry. Her grumpy old grandmother was nowhere to be seen. The house was about as welcoming as a prison. She was lonely and fed up and tired. She would escape. It was the only reasonable thing to do.

The old-fashioned stories about treasure on islands were obviously bunkum. Islands were filled with horrible people and horribly boring things. She would ask Rowan to get her off the island in his kayak. It was an excellent plan!

Chapter Six

The Storm

Elen tossed and turned in a sea of angry spume, her boat thrown about on the ocean like a matchstick. All she could see were mountainous waves. The only sign of land was a huge jagged lump of rock that towered into the swirling black sky. The whole world was drowning. She was losing her footing. The boat was being smashed against the rocks. She managed to claw onto the breaking boat with her fingers, her

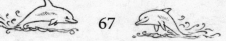

nails, her teeth, fighting with every ounce of her strength against the dragging waves. Elen screamed, 'Help me!' but her voice made no sound.

She shot up with a start. Her quilt was wrapped tightly around her foot, her pillows scattered the floor. She had sweat on her forehead and she could taste its saltiness on her lips. She wanted her mum. It took her a few seconds to remember she was on the island.

The weather outside had changed from bad to horrific.

A gale-force wind howled against the windows and screeched through the fireplace. Branches thrashed into The Lanterns, as if trying to knock it to the ground. The entire house clanked and shuddered and groaned. The windows rattled as if the ghosts of a million dead pirates were struggling to get in.

There was a dazzling flash of electric blue light. Elen held her breath and counted. One, two, three. She closed her eyes tight, drawing the quilt up around her knees. Four, five…

'BANG!' The noise of the thunder made her jump out of her skin. Then there was a crash, even louder than the thunder. Elen screamed and leapt out of bed. She didn't care how miserable or terrible Gran was; she had to make sure she was OK. She raced down the landing and rapped at her grandmother's bedroom door. Nothing. She pushed it open and saw an empty bed.

Elen's first thought was that Gran must have gone downstairs to investigate the crash. Her second thought was that her grandmother was selfish not to check on her first. Elen tried to shout louder than the thunder and the clatter of debris in the yard.

'Gran!' she yelled.

She rushed down the stairs and stopped at the bottom.

The front door was wide open.

A bolt of lightning hit the ground at the end of the lane.

'Gran!' she shouted again at the top of her lungs. 'Where are you?'

There was no reply. Elen rushed from room to room throwing the light switches on. 'Gran!' she yelled, hurting her throat.

Another bolt of lightning slashed the sky, closer now and even more threatening. Elen saw a face in the gloom and screamed.

She came to her senses. It was her own face in the mirror. She needed to calm down. She needed to breathe.

'BOOM!' A stupendous bolt of lightning followed by a violent roll of thunder made her

heart race. Elen bit her lip to prevent herself from screaming again.

She was going to have to go outside. Gran was nowhere to be seen. Of all the stupid things to do, Elen raged. Going out into a storm all alone! What was she thinking?

She shrugged her mackintosh on. She considered her wellingtons but nobody can run properly in wellies however hard they try, so she put on her normal shoes, scratching the back of her heel. There was no time to search for a torch and she had no idea where to start looking. Elen grabbed her map and dashed out into the spiteful night.

If things had seemed bad from the inside, outside they were worse. Trees had been wrenched up by the wind. Their roots stuck up into the air like skeleton fingers. Lightning flashes split the sky and made the world look

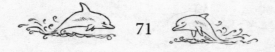

like an old-fashioned negative she'd once seen in a museum.

Elen sped down the pitch-black lane. The track was alive with water and mud. The current dragged at her feet, splashed up her legs, pulled at her. The rain was torrential and it took only seconds for her map to be drenched. As it was way too dark to read it anyway, she stuffed it into the pool of water collecting in her pocket and kept on running.

'Think, Elen, think,' she shouted out loud. Her voice was swallowed by the gale. She imagined it hurtling across the sea and hammering against the shutters of Aberglad.

The lighthouse swept the road (which was more like a gushing river) in bands of bright white light. Elen stumbled when the light disappeared and sped up again when it came back.

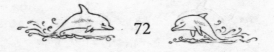

Something was calling her deep inside. Tugging at her memory and trying to tell her a really important thing.

She wiped the water from her eyes and stopped. The storm buffeted her from side to side.

Her grandfather. It was something about him, she was sure of it.

Elen squeezed her eyes tight shut and thought back. She pictured her mother. Thankfully she didn't have the sunglasses on this time. She heard her mother's voice whispering a name that she couldn't quite catch hold of.

'Jack.' Her mother repeated, 'Jack, Jack, Jack.'

That was it! The name on the bench was her grandfather's name. But her grandmother couldn't have gone up there, surely?

Elen knew immediately that she had.

Anything could happen to her – she could fall

and break her leg. She could be blown over the edge into the hungry sea.

Elen ran towards the lighthouse, its huge lens a giant Cyclops eye roaming the pitch-black night, searching for prey.

She reached the path down to the bench. It was completely dark and even more terrifying than she remembered. Adrenalin pumped through her. She could slip and be dashed to smithereens on the cliffs below.

Using the beam from the lighthouse, she tried to be as safe as she could. She stood like a statue when it was dark and moved as swiftly as possible when the beams came around again. Soon she was out of range of the lighthouse and had to feel her way along the path in complete darkness.

'Gran!' Elen shouted, even though the roar of the waves on the rocks below was deafening and she knew there was no hope of her being heard.

Another fork of lightning split the night and suddenly Elen could see her grandmother against the swallowing sky, her hair tugging at her skull in the wind, her hands raised to the clouds.

'Jack!' her grandmother cried.

Elen raced to her and threw her arms around her.

'What are you doing up here?' she yelled but her voice was drowned out.

Gran sank into her arms like a rag doll. Elen had to struggle to support her.

'Pull yourself together!' Elen yelled.

Her grandmother leaned so hard against her that she threatened to topple them both over the edge.

Elen grabbed Gran's elbow and dragged her firmly back towards the lighthouse. The woman put up no fight. All the energy had drained out of her fragile body.

It took an eternity to lead her back, but eventually Elen could make out the lights she had left on in The Lanterns. She managed to get her inside and up to her bedroom. They were both soaked through and shivering.

'Turn out the lights!' Gran shrieked, almost scaring Elen out of her wits.

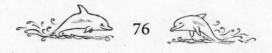

'OK, calm down,' Elen said. 'I'll turn out the lights and you put some warm clothes on.'

Elen ran about the house switching out the lights then rushed to dry herself and change before she got hypothermia. When she went back to her grandmother's bedroom, the old woman was lying on the bed mumbling.

'Lost at sea,' she mumbled fretfully. 'Never light the lanterns.'

In her hand she clutched the beautiful box.

Elen stroked her grandmother's head until she began to calm down.

She looked sadly at Elen. 'They didn't want to leave you. You know that, don't you? They're trying to get work. They had no choice.' She drifted off into a doze.

Elen wondered what she meant. Who hadn't wanted to leave her? Who had to work? As she examined Gran's face, looking for similarities to

 77

her mother, she realised. Her parents had gone abroad to find work, not on a holiday. They didn't want Elen to worry and they must feel guilty about leaving her. Elen knew that money was short and they'd been arguing about it. She slotted the pieces of the unhappy puzzle together as her grandmother slept, her hair curling as it dried.

When she was properly asleep, the box slipped from her fingers. Elen picked it up.

She felt absolutely wretched that she'd had such nasty thoughts about her mum and dad. They could have told her the truth, but they must have thought she was too young to understand. She felt sad and useless.

She rubbed her fingers over the box, wondering what was inside. She was fed up of secrets. It wasn't exactly the right thing to do, but she might have saved her grandmother's life and perhaps she deserved a small reward. It

couldn't do any harm. Elen held her breath and unhooked the elaborate clasp.

There was nothing inside but a bunch of boring old photographs.

Disappointed, Elen flicked through them silently. What made them so special that her grandmother had to keep them a secret? Old people were so weird.

As if she could hear Elen's thoughts, Gran rolled over with a loud sigh. Startled, Elen dropped the photographs all over the floor. She was putting them back when she noticed that one had writing on the back.

Growing life and magic true
Of beauteous lights of fire
Love's treasures then will come to you
Deliver heart's desire

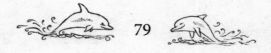

It was signed in old-style script, *Blackbeard*.

A tiny spark of hope flickered inside Elen. Perhaps there was treasure. This photograph had practically fallen into her lap and it seemed to be a clue to something. What if she could find it? What if she found some wonderful gold or jewels and her parents' money worries were solved and they wouldn't have to work away from home? If only she could work out the meaning of the rhyme. It must be a clue to somewhere on the island. She needed to find it and then perhaps, just perhaps, her family would be rich beyond their wildest dreams.

Elen placed the box on the bedside table but she kept the photograph. She knew that stealing was wrong, but this was only borrowing. Elen was going to find the treasure if it was the last thing she did.

Chapter Seven

The Mysterious Photograph

Elen inspected the photograph in the morning light.

It was brown and cream and curled at the edges. She assumed it must have been black and white once but had faded over time.

The picture was of a garden. Lights were strung up across leafy trees. Pretty flowers grew

81

everywhere. There were lots of people in the garden all doing different things, Elen looked in amazement from one to the other. At the centre there were two people waltzing. The man and woman looked into each other's eyes. Another man sat further back watching the dancing couple.

Elen would bet that a moment after this photo was taken the dancing couple had kissed. She was glad it was just a picture so that they couldn't. She hated all that kissing stuff.

She wondered who the people were and where the beautiful garden was.

At the left-hand side of the photo there was a woman, her face turned away from the camera. She looked as if she was clapping from the way her hands were held up in the air. Her dress was in mid sway and her beautiful hair tumbled over her shoulders. Elen bet that she wouldn't have a Frankenstein fringe if she turned round.

Most strangely of all, she could see someone mostly hidden underneath the table. They appeared to be trying to grab something tiny, which might be a hen pecking at the ground nearby. It seemed a very peculiar thing to be doing at a party. Who would do something like that?

It came to Elen in a flash.

'I want to tell you about my hen collection,' the candyfloss-on-legs had said.

Elen scrutinised the tiny piece of face she could see. It had to be her.

Elen congratulated herself. She had always fancied being a detective and had been told by lots of people that she had 'an enquiring mind'. She had been told by lots of other people that she was 'easily distracted by irrelevant questions' but she preferred the first opinion.

She ran her fingers over the slanted writing.

How was she going to find where the treasure was buried? It might be at the bottom of a glassy pool. It could be buried deep under the sand on Blackbeard's Bay. Perhaps that was how the bay got its name. Elen felt the hairs on the back of her neck prickle. She would have to try her best. She would also need help from someone who knew the island like the back of their hand. There was only one person who could help her and she didn't really want to ask him, with him being so pompous and everything, but she couldn't see she had a choice.

Pulling her fringe down as far as it would go (which wasn't far) she crept across the landing to check that her grandmother was still asleep. The old woman lay there, her hair falling across the pillow like sea waves, her breathing soft and steady. She wouldn't be awake for hours.

Excellent, Elen thought. Plenty of time for a

 84

bit of detective work. Elen stifled a yawn. She was tired from her night-time adventures but nothing was going to prevent her investigations.

The morning was crisp and bright. The tangy smell of the sea was salty strong on the air. Cobwebs held heavy drops like diamonds and spiders busied themselves with repairs to their homes. An upturned umbrella flapped and *scraggled* in the breeze, its metal skeleton caught by a branch, like a colourful bird wanting to fly. The sun cast a weak lemony light over the mess the storm had created. Blackbirds hopped along the path scavenging for food and gulls swooped in arcs across the fresh clean sky.

Elen wasn't sure where to find Rowan. She didn't fancy the forest and didn't want to relive the lighthouse path just yet. So she decided to try the beach where she had met him fishing.

The storm had dug great rivulets in the sands.

Water trickled down them to the waves. Large clumps of frothy foam blew about as if someone had added washing-up liquid to the sea. Smashed crab shells and pincers were strewn all over the beach and big clumps of blue and green netting had been washed ashore.

Elen jumped the tiny streams and collected a few purple mussel shells. A crow dropped a shellfish onto a rock and dived down to eat the fleshy insides.

Miraculously the boy was in exactly the same place on the rocks as before, Captain Beaky at his side as ever with his mouth full of tiny fish. The boy was staring at something through binoculars.

'Hello,' she said shyly, half afraid he would be nasty to her again and tell her off for making a noise.

'Oh, hi.' He pointed out to a rock exposed by

the low tide. 'Cormorant. They hold their wings out like that to dry them.'

Elen looked at the big black bird, wondering why everyone here was so obsessed with birds (though she had to admit the puffin was fascinating). She asked casually, 'I was just wondering if you could help me with something?'

'Is it repairing the damage from last night? I'm very good at fixing things. The telegraph wires have fallen down in Aberglad and a tree blew into one of the windows on Winkle Cottage. Nerys is really annoyed. We are lucky the lighthouse didn't snap in two, the wind was so strong.'

He saw the alarmed look on Elen's face.

'Joke. Lighthouses are circular so that they can take more of a bashing from a storm. Was it brilliant or what?'

Elen wondered how much she should tell him. 'It was interesting.'

He seemed satisfied with this. They both watched the cormorant hold its wings high up to the sun. The cormorant wasn't entirely boring, Elen decided, as the water ran off its back in crystal twinkles. Captain Beaky hopped about as if he could read her thoughts and approved.

'I just wondered,' Elen went on, 'if you were any good at understanding poetry?'

'Of course. I am absolutely brilliant at it. When I can be bothered.' He didn't even lower his binoculars.

'It's just that it's really important and...'

'Why?'

'Because. Well. Just because. That's all.' Elen tried to keep her voice light. She didn't plan to share her fortune with Rowan when she found it.

He was interested now. He let the binoculars hang from his neck. 'Because what?'

'It's not really any of your business.'

'Well, I'll just go then.' He turned to scramble over the rocks away from her.

'No. Wait. OK. As long as you promise not to tell anyone.'

'Of course I won't.'

Elen wondered if she could trust him. She decided she didn't have much choice.

She took the photo carefully out of her pocket and showed him the reverse.

His eyes lit up with excitement as he slowly sounded the words out.

> *Growing life and magic true*
> *Of beauteous lights of fire*
> *Love's treasures then will come to you*
> *Deliver heart's desire*

 89

'Blackbeard.' He read the signature and then stared in astonishment at Elen. 'Blackbeard was a pirate.'

'I know that.' Elen wished she hadn't had to ask for help. 'Anyway, it's not important at all. Just one of those things.'

'You made it sound pretty important before. I think it's a kind of treasure map. There are lots of old stories about this island and treasure.'

The boy was too sharp.

'Look, it might lead to something and it might not, OK?' Elen replied. 'If you could tell me where this place is or who these people are, we might have our first clue.'

'I don't know any of them,' Rowan said.

'None of them?' Elen was dismayed. 'If you look carefully under the table, I think that I met this woman in Aberglad.'

Rowan studied it. 'Sally! It's her.' He jumped.

'And this in the background is Captain Evans! You can tell from the way he is scratching his chin.'

Elen snatched the picture. He was right. When she looked very closely she could see that it was a much younger Mr Evans. She was quite cross with herself for not realising straight away.

'There's his boat now. Let's go and ask him about it.' Rowan picked the puffin up gently and put him in his pocket, so that only his clown-like face poked out.

'OK, but don't show him the rhyme or he'll try to get the treasure first.' Elen was always told that she could be bossy. She liked to think of it as having leadership skills.

'Like I would be that stupid,' Rowan said. 'He'd want to take all the good stuff for himself. And it should just be shared between the two of us.'

 91

Elen bristled. But she decided she would fight about it with Rowan when they actually found something.

'Captain Evans!' Rowan shouted.

'Ah, it's Able Seaman Elen and Able Seaman Rowan.' He smiled. 'What a lovely day for sailing, if you fancy it?'

On another day Elen might have wanted to go for a glide across the beautiful azure water, now that she had been brave enough to go out once. Today the treasure was far more important.

'Thanks Mr Evans…' she began.

'That's Captain Evans, if you don't mind.' He winked. 'Obey the rules, Able Seaman Elen or I'll make you walk the plank.'

'That's Able Seawoman Elen, if you don't mind,' Elen retaliated.

He creased up with laughter. 'Fair play. Of course it is. I stand corrected.'

'We were just wondering if you know who these people are? We can see that one of them is you so we thought you might remember this party? Or anything special about it?' Elen stopped herself from rambling on before she sounded suspicious. She held the photo out to him but kept tight hold of it, in case he turned it around, and added, 'Not that it is very important or anything.'

'No, it's just a rubbishy old photo and we're a bit bored, that's all.' Rowan yawned. Elen stretched her arms in the air as if she too was ready for bed. Rowan and Elen exchanged glances. They were partners in crime.

Captain Evans took a long slow breath in.

'I was quite the handsome young man then, wasn't I?'

Elen and Rowan exchanged glances again.

'That was a magical afternoon. Your grandmother cast a spell over everyone there.'

 93

'My grandmother?' Elen asked, confused.

'Of course. That's your grandmother and that's your grandfather.' He pointed to the couple dancing. Elen could hardly believe her eyes. 'And this of course is your mother, Able Seaman ... er ... Seawoman Elen.'

Elen looked at the woman clapping in astonishment. She was about to ask lots of questions about her family when Rowan butted in. 'How interesting,' he said in an uninterested voice. 'I wonder where it was taken?' he asked as if he didn't really care about the answer.

Captain Evans tutted. 'Young people don't use their eyes anymore. That's the garden at The Lanterns. It's Elen's grandmother's garden.'

If Elen's eyes had been wide open before, they could have come out on stalks now. This beautiful, light-filled, well-tended garden was that dump of a yard at the back of Gran's house? She couldn't believe it!

'Your grandmother gave up on a lot of things when your grandfather was lost at sea.' Captain Evans looked forlorn.

'Thanks very much.' Rowan snatched the photo out of Elen's hands and ran off.

'Yes thanks,' Elen said politely before running straight after him.

When she caught him up, she grabbed him roughly by the shoulder. 'Oy. Where do you think you are going?' She tussled the picture out of his hands.

 95

'It's an acrostic. I noticed it when Captain Evans was holding the photo up to his face and we could only see the back.' He shook all over with excitement.

'I don't care what it is. You don't run off with my photo.'

'Stop whinging and look. We did them in school. The letters at the beginning of each line spell out a word. See for yourself.'

Growing life and magic true
Of beauteous lights of fire
Love's treasures then will come to you
Deliver heart's desire

Elen looked at the first letters: G. O. L. D. They spelled GOLD!

Chapter Eight

Plotting

'We have to get her out of the house,' Rowan urged. 'Then we can look for the treasure.'

To their dismay, even though Gran usually spent her days out of the cottage, she was currently entrenched in the kitchen surrounded by weird ingredients, chatting about the tides to Blackbeard as if he were answering back. She looked set to be there for hours.

Elen, Rowan and Captain Beaky sat on the stoop.

'How can we get her out?' Rowan looked at Elen expectantly.

Elen bit the inside of her mouth as she tried to think of a genius plan. Nothing came.

'What is she interested in?' Rowan asked.

'I've no idea. Since I've been here all she's done is talk to dead pirates and babble on about me keeping my nose out.'

'There must be something else. Think, Elen, think,' Rowan said, using the phrase she often said to herself.

She repeated it quietly, 'Think, Elen, think.'

The only thing she could think of was that her grandmother insisted that mermaids could be spotted off Seal Point, which was obviously ridiculous. She told Rowan this pathetic piece of information.

'Genius.' He gazed at Elen as if she was a magician. 'Utter genius!'

'What is?'

'The mermaids. We'll say they've been seen again.'

'What do you mean *again*? There's no such thing as mermaids!'

'Of course there isn't. But there have been loads of sightings here. People bring their boats out to search for them and everything. It's died down a bit now but some people still believe they are here. Lots of strange things happen in Wales…'

'So people keep telling me.' Elen picked up Captain Beaky and planted a kiss on his feathered head.

'Come on!' Rowan rushed in through the front door of The Lanterns. He pretended to vomit at the terrible green smell of the mixture bubbling on the stove. Then he shouted to Elen's grandmother, 'Mrs Thomas, the mermaids have been seen again!'

Gran got up from her chair, where she'd been crushing lavender with a pestle and mortar, and turned off the flame under the pot. She stopped. With one arm in one sleeve of her cardigan, she turned to Rowan.

'The mermaids?'

'Yes,' Rowan answered, squirming a little.

She put her other arm through the other armhole. Then she stopped again.

'There has been another sighting of real mermaids?'

Elen's grandmother stared straight into Rowan's face. He shrank back a little but still managed a nod.

'Well, I'd better be off then. Stay away from the cooker. I'll see you later.' She put her hand to her mouth, almost as if she was hiding a giggle. 'Or do you want to come with me?'

Rowan looked at Elen in panic.

'I don't believe in mermaids,' Elen replied, looking straight at her. It wasn't a lie. Of course she didn't believe in mermaids. That was just kids' stuff.

'Young people. Never believe in anything

anymore. Come on, Blackbeard.' Gran grabbed her stick and a camera and hobble-ran out of the house.

They watched her disappear down the lane.

'What is that green stuff she's cooking?' Rowan's face had a distinctly yellow pallor.

'I think it must be some kind of witches' brew to ward off evil.' Elen pulled a face.

'She's weird,' Rowan said happily.

'Not as weird as you,' Elen chortled.

They waited a few minutes to make sure Gran didn't get suspicious and turn around, then raced into the back garden.

It was even messier than Elen remembered. The brambles were strangling the life out of everything. New weeds had sprouted up everywhere and an inexplicable green slime had appeared on the walls.

Rowan stopped in his tracks. 'Do you think Captain Evans is right that this is the same garden?'

They compared the photo with the state of the garden now. There were definite similarities if you used your imagination. But you REALLY had to use your imagination.

'Come on! Let's start searching.'

Elen placed Captain Beaky carefully on the floor and they searched under the upturned plant pots, putting them the right way up along

103

the way. They tore the weeds up with their bare hands, hoping to find the handle of a barely hidden chest. They sliced their fingers and wrists pulling brambles apart, looking for a secret door.

The garden looked significantly better. But there was no sign of the treasure. They were exhausted, muddy and the light was getting dim. Miserable, they went back into the kitchen where the scent of the concoction lingered

horribly. Captain Beaky walked slowly across the table-top and hid his face in the flowers as if he was trying to block out the smell.

They put the rhyme on the kitchen table and sat down, supporting their heads in their earth-covered hands and stretching their aching necks. The sun began to sink outside.

> *Growing life and magic true*
> *Of beauteous lights of fire*
> *Love's treasures then will come to you*
> *Deliver heart's desire*

She looked at the signature 'Blackbeard' and imagined the ancient pirate sailing the seven seas and collecting jewels.

'We must be missing something.' Elen concentrated hard on the rhyme. '*Growing life and magic true*. What could that mean?'

'Search me.' Rowan looked despondent.

'*Growing life.* It could be a baby.'

'Great – where are we going to get one of those?' Rowan was sulking.

'Well, you're acting like one. Perhaps you'll do?' Elen wasn't about to put up with his moodiness. 'It could be plants.'

Rowan sat up. 'Go on.'

'Growing life could be something to do with the plants and flowers in the picture.'

He was very interested again now. 'What about the rest of it?'

'I'm not sure about the *Beauteous lights of fire* bit.'

Rowan jumped up out of his seat. 'It's all the lights in the picture. Look, there are fairy lights and candles and all sorts.'

'Brilliant. Perhaps the treasure hasn't been found because my grandmother keeps it so stupidly dark here.' Elen was getting excited. She

carried on reading it aloud. '*Love's treasure then will come to you*

Deliver heart's desire.'

'Of course!' Rowan was hopping about like mad. '*Love's treasure* – it means gold. People always give each other gold stuff when they are in love. You've seen all that gross stuff on TV.'

He got down on one knee and pretended to propose to someone. 'Will you marry me?'

'Bleurch,' Elen said.

'And then they give each other rings and stuff made of gold. G.O.L.D.'

He was right. Elen felt her heart pounding. 'So it's here somewhere. But where?'

'That's the magic bit. We have to get flowers growing in the garden. We have to fill the garden with lights. And then we wait.'

'Wait for what?'

'For a sign.'

'How's that going to happen?'

'I don't know. Perhaps the lights will show up something or the shadows of the flowers will fall where the treasure is buried or the light will lift a dark curse that's been out on the land or … I don't know, but we have to listen to the rhyme and believe in "magic true" just like it says.' He was so excited he stood on the chair and then jumped up onto the table, scattering bits of lavender all over the floor and frightening Captain Beaky who gave an excited hop. 'We have to recreate the garden in this photo so that the magic will work. But we can't tell another living soul about it. Pact?'

He put his hand up.

Elen copied him solemnly. 'Pact,' she repeated.

Chapter Nine

The Cave

Elen read the list they had written.

1. Plants.
2. Decorations.
3. Lights
4. More lights.

'How are we supposed to get these things?' Elen sat at the top of a golden sand dune feeling the

prickly grasses with her hand. 'We can't steal stuff or dig plants up on the island.'

Rowan sifted sand through his fingers and watched it trickle onto his leg. Captain Beaky threw up bits of sand with his webbed feet. 'We'll have to ask for help.'

'Duh. I don't know anyone here, in case you hadn't noticed. Besides, people are nosy. They want to know everything about everyone, Nerys told me.'

'We'll tell them that we are doing a nice thing for your grandmother. We could be cleaning up the garden so that she can enjoy it in her old age. That'll impress people.' He carried on trickling sand, putting a stray ant to one side so that he wouldn't hurt it.

Elen chewed the inside of her cheek and thought it over. 'It's not a bad plan.'

'It's the only plan we've got.'

Elen thought of how much had happened since she first arrived in Aberglad. She thought about her trip with Nerys. She wondered when Nerys would leave Winkle Cottage to visit her.

'That's it!' She snapped her fingers with excitement. 'Winkle Cottage has got loads of flowers in the garden. I bet Nerys would give us some.'

'Excellent,' Rowan agreed. 'I'll ask her when I go home.'

Elen realised Rowan had never mentioned his home before. She wondered how to approach the subject without seeming nosy.

'Do you live near Nerys then?' She pretended to be more interested in plaiting the golden grasses together.

'Just around the corner.' He threw the sand in his palm down and stood with his back to her.

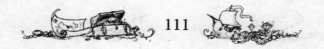

Even though he clearly didn't want to talk about it, Elen went on, 'Why do you spend so much time here if you live there?'

She could see Rowan's frame stiffen.

'There's no one home much.'

'Why?' Elen sometimes couldn't help herself from asking questions.

'My parents just aren't all that interested, that's all. Are we going to get on with finding the gold?' He picked up Captain Beaky and marched away from Elen.

She thought about her mum and dad again. They tried so hard to make things good for her. She wished she could give them a massive hug and apologise for being such a brat. Swallowing the lump in her throat, she called after Rowan, 'Wait for me then!'

When she caught up with him his face was crimson and he avoided making eye contact.

112

'What are we going to do about lights? I don't have any money. Do you?' she asked.

'Of course I don't.'

Elen recoiled at the nastiness in his voice. He saw her reaction and softened a little. 'It's OK. We'll make our own. Here. You can carry Captain Beaky. Come on.'

He led her toward the lighthouse and then down a steep, windy path to Smugglers' Rocks. The sea was so calm it looked like a mirror for the clouds in the distance and it had a silken sheen close up.

Puffins landed on it, breaking its stillness with their orange webbed feet and watching her with their beady black eyes.

'Look, Captain Beaky, that's what you are going to do when you are better.' Elen could have sworn that the puffin winked at her. She couldn't stop herself from laughing out loud. She hoped

that she wouldn't one day find herself doing impressions of birds on crowded trains.

The puffins floated out to sea as the water tugged and frothed against the jagged rocks.

'Look at this.' Rowan showed her a rock pool full of anemones. She touched them gently and watched them recoil into blobs like jelly sweets. Water snails left trails at the bottom of the pool and tiny shrimps darted about.

After a while Elen noticed how quiet it was and looked up from the underwater world. Rowan had disappeared.

She shielded her eyes with her hand. 'Rowan?' There was no answer.

She called out loudly, 'Rowan, where are you?'

Her gaze skimmed the surface of the sea. Perhaps he had dived in for a swim. He was nowhere to be seen. 'Rowan!'

Elen scooped Captain Beaky up and

scrambled over the rocks to get a higher vantage point, scraping her leg on the barnacles. She was going to have to call out a lifeboat if she couldn't find him really soon. Her swimming was strong because she'd had lessons and practised lots, but it might be hard if he'd been washed too far out. Panic spread through her body like wildfire.

Balancing on top of the highest rock, she yelled at the very top of her voice, 'ROWWWWWWAAAAANNNNNNNN!'

'What's all the fuss about?' His head popped up from a crevice in the cliff behind her.

'Where were you?' Elen tried not to show how afraid she had been. She could feel her legs trembling and her breathing was out of control.

'Did I scare you? Sorry.' Rowan looked genuinely rueful. 'I brought you here to show you something. I just wanted to check it out first.'

'Well, you could have warned me. Captain Beaky thought something had happened to you.' Elen was surprised by how upset she was.

'Sorry. I didn't think.' He examined a piece of rock closely. 'I'm not used to having friends.'

She forgave him at once. She wasn't used to having many friends either. 'It's OK. What did you want to show me?'

He beckoned her into a small cleft in the cliff. The low passageway in the rock opened up into a giant cave.

Stalactites hung dripping from the ceiling and stalagmites grew up like fairy towers to meet them.

'Watch you don't fall in!' Rowan took Captain Beaky and held Elen's arm as she walked towards a huge hole in the cave's floor. It looked as if it went down for miles.

'Phew. Thanks for saving me.'

She wondered why Rowan was chuckling at her.
'Watch this.' He took a pebble out of his
pocket and threw it into the hole. Elen waited to
see how far down it would drop and gasped as
it hit the centre of the hole and sent concentric
ripples outwards. It wasn't a hole but a huge pool

of water. The water reflected the ceiling of the cave so clearly that it looked as if it was an upside down cavern in front of them.

Elen punched Rowan on the arm. 'I thought I was going to fall in, you idiot.'

'Well, you might have got very wet!' He howled with laughter. It echoed around the cave, sounding as though there were twenty Rowans enjoying the joke.

Captain Beaky made a low growling noise that was somewhere between a chainsaw and a cow mooing.

Elen laughed. 'That's all very well but it isn't helping us find the treasure.'

'That's where you're wrong. Just you wait.' He disappeared out of the cave, leaving Elen standing in the dim light alone. She tried not to think about the ghosts of drowned pirates who might be hidden at the bottom of the pool. It was quite

echo-y and lonely down here. There were different paths leading off in various directions. Elen peered into their seemingly never-ending blackness and imagined a labyrinth just out of sight where a person might lose their way forever if they took a wrong turn. The sea might gush in and fill the cave to its roof.

Thankfully Rowan reappeared. 'Give it a minute till the sun hits the right place.'

They waited, listening to the sound of their own breathing, the drips falling lazily from the cavern roof, the gentle slip-slap of waves outside.

'Here we go.' Rowan looked up at a small hole which Elen hadn't noticed before. It looked out at the dazzling blue sky above them. It seemed to be filling with light. 'That's the sun moving into the right spot.'

Elen squinted at it. It hurt the back of her eyeballs.

119

'Don't look at that. Look at this!' Rowan sounded elated. Elen turned.

The cave was filled with dancing lights. Lights bent and squiggled and waltzed and scurried across the walls. They wobbled and *wibbled* and shimmied.

'It's the effect of sunlight on water. We can make our own lights if we get bowls of water and put them in the right places in the garden.'

'It's magical.' Elen whispered. They watched the performance of the lights for a few moments in silence.

Captain Beaky took the opportunity to have a splash about in the sunlit pool.

'Will that be enough?' Rowan wondered out loud. 'Perhaps we need to think of other stuff.'

'What about CDs?' Elen remembered something her mother had shown her.

'Do we need music?' Rowan looked perplexed.

'No, I mean to make lights. We could hang them from the trees so that the sun bounces off them.'

'That's brilliant. I've got a few old ones I can bring.'

'They make good decorations too.' Elen stated feeling quite proud.

Rowan looked at the photo. 'We can make other decorations...' he began.

'String shells together to make garlands!' Elen interrupted.

'Collect sea glass to make colourful patterns,' Rowan went on.

'What's sea glass?' Elen asked. It wasn't so difficult to admit she didn't know everything about islands now that they were friends.

'It's glass that has been washed into the sea and rubbed smooth by the waves. If we could think of a way to hang it up, we could get the

light to shine through it. Like a stained-glass window.'

'That would be amazing and I think I have just the thing!' Elen squealed, hopping about with happiness. 'We need to get going. I'll start gathering stuff for decorations.'

'And I'll get a message to Nerys about flowers.'

'We'll meet at The Lanterns tomorrow morning and get it set up!'

'Brilliant.'

'I'll get rid of my grandmother.'

'Even more brilliant!'

In the whirling watery light of the cave, magic seemed so close you could almost reach out and take a bite of it. The treasure was almost in their grasp.

Chapter Ten

Preparations

They decided to put the plan into action as quickly as possible. If they were going to recreate the photograph, they would need to get Elen's grandmother out of the way again.

Elen practised reasons Gran should leave the house in the mirror.

'It's a lovely day, Grandmother. I think you'd be doing your health some good if you went out for a very long walk.'

Her reflection looked as innocent as an angel. She tried it again in an even more angelic voice and decided she would cut the 'very long' bit as it might sound suspicious.

Elen had been up since dawn scouring the beach for sea glass and picking up purple and blue mussel shells and white and peach whelk shells. She'd found a fossil with an ammonite on it too, but was keeping that to show to her mum and dad when they got back.

Gran stood on the front doorstep looking out at the sea. 'Lovely morning for it, Blackbeard,' she said loudly.

Elen wondered what it was a lovely morning for. She supposed it was a lovely morning for lots of things. She reminded herself to focus on the task in hand.

She sidled up to her grandmother. 'Ooh what a fantastic day. Walk. You. Good walk.'

It didn't come out exactly as she'd planned.

'Chance would be a fine thing.' Gran buttoned up her overcoat and grabbed the handle of a shopping bag on wheels. 'I've got to get over to Aberglad to get some supplies. Food doesn't grow on trees, you know.'

'Well, some of it does,' Elen couldn't help replying.

'You're right. But not in my garden.' Her grandmother looked sorrowful. 'Right. I'll be back before dark.'

'How long before dark?' Elen panicked.

'Last boat comes over as the sun goes down. I'll be on it. You keep the lights low here. Save electric.' She started to make her way down the lane then stopped. 'You can come with me if you want to? If you're afraid of the dark?'

'No, I'd much rather stay here. I'm not afraid.

125

Honestly.' Elen could feel her heart beating wildly in her throat.

Gran smiled. 'There's nothing to be afraid of here. As long as you're sure?'

'Absolutely.' Elen used her sweetest voice.

'Just like your mother.' The woman sauntered off chuckling. She glanced back. 'Might have a surprise for you when I come back.'

For a moment, she thought her grandmother meant the garden – that she knew they would have a surprise for her – and panicked. Then she stopped herself. Gran probably meant a present from the market or something. She gave her grandmother's back a smile and went inside.

Elen shut the door then spread her collection out on the kitchen table.

She held a piece of pale smooth sea glass up to her eye and the world went watery green. She inspected her other findings.

Not long till Rowan would be here with some plants and they could start.

Elen wondered whether the gold would be chunky coins or goblets encrusted with emeralds. Perhaps there would be some beautifully designed cutlasses that she could practise sword fighting with. She imagined herself sailing the seas and fighting off evil forces.

There was a rapid knock at the front door. Elen ran to it. 'Who is it?' she called through the wood.

'It's me. Rowan.'

Elen let out a sigh of relief and turned the handle. The sight before her was a huge surprise.

Not only was Rowan there, with his arms full of CDs and balls of string, but Captain Evans stood with him, a spade in his hand. Nerys peered out from behind the most potted plants

it was humanly possible to hold and Sally, the woman Elen had met on her first day in Aberglad, chased a couple of squawking hens up and down the lane. Captain Beaky made a noise like a door squeaking by way of hello.

'We wanted to help.' Captain Evans blurted out. 'We thought it was such a nice thing to do. Sorting out the old boot's garden. We thought we'd give you a hand. We had to hide from the battleaxe down by the beach so she wouldn't spot us. It was a bit hairy, I can tell you. I've got seeds for the vegetable patch and I've paid someone to run my boat today.'

'And I've got flowers,' Nerys said from behind her armful of pots, getting a petal stuck in her mouth.

'And I've brought hens for free-range eggs!' Sally called, holding one hen nestled under her arm as she tried to catch the other.

Elen looked slyly at Rowan. He gave a small surreptitious shake of his head. Then they didn't know about the treasure. They'd believed the story of just trying to help.

'Let's get to work then!' Captain Evans

blustered into the house, pranging the salted clock with his spade. It started ticking.

'Time for a change!' he exclaimed.

They all went through to the kitchen. 'Good grief. What's that pong?' Captain Evans said, waving his hand in front of his nose.

Elen pointed to the green gloop in embarrassment. 'I don't know what it is but I'm sorry.'

'Ah! The island's fabulous ointment. You might think it's smelly but it makes a wonderful job of keeping skin healthy. This is a really well-known island recipe that only uses natural ingredients. It's like medicine for skin,' Nerys explained.

'It isn't some terrible spell to ward off evil spirits?' Rowan asked, getting himself a kick from Elen.

'Ha! No. Mrs Thomas sells it to the tourists

on Aberglad. How else do you think she makes enough money to get by? Though if you want the truth, I think she's is making it in case your grandfather ever comes back, so she can still look the same.' A sadness fell over the gathering.

'He's not coming back?' Elen whispered. 'My grandfather. He isn't ever coming back.'

Nerys gave her a cuddle and kissed the crown of her head. 'No,' she said softly. 'Come on. Let's get on with this garden.'

They shuffled outside.

'Blimey, what a mess,' Sally grumbled, the two hens wriggling for freedom in her arms. 'This is going to take some work.'

'We'd better get a move on then.' Captain Evans dug his spade into the ground. 'What's the plan, Elen?'

They all stared at her. Even the hens stopped

131

clucking and watched her. Captain Beaky wandered around as if he was making decisions on what he was going to tidy.

Elen wasn't used to being in charge, but there was no time to waste if they were going to get everything finished and find the riches.

'Well, that might be a good spot for the vegetable patch.' Elen tried to make her voice sound stronger than she felt. 'Then maybe the plants could go around here.' She pointed to the borders of the garden.

Everyone nodded.

'Perhaps the hens could live in this part of the garden where they have sun and shade and can run around lots?'

'Brilliant,' Sally said. 'They'll love it. I'll just move all this rubbish away in the wheelbarrow first.'

'I'll get to work on the digging.' Captain Evans started on the vegetable patch.

132

'And I'll get these plants bedded in.' Nerys winked at Elen. 'Good job, Elen.'

'Thanks.' Elen blushed. 'We'll get on with the decorations.'

Rowan and Elen sped into the kitchen and shut the door.

'I WAS AFRAID TO SAY ANYTHING. I'm completely busting with excitement!' Rowan began loudly then changed his voice to a tiny whisper. 'I thought that if I opened my mouth I'd just scream out TREASURE and then we'd be completely scuppered. I'm no good at secrets. That's why everyone is here. I just had to tell some people.'

He was crestfallen and Elen took pity on him.

'You won't have to keep quiet for too long. With this much help, the magic will work all the quicker. We need to get these decorations done. Bowls for water.'

'Check.' Rowan started to fill the bowls with water from the tap. 'We can tell that lot they are for the birds to drink.'

'I've got shells to make garlands to hang in the trees. They just need to be threaded onto this.' Elen showed Rowan pieces of string and a needle. 'I only picked up ones with holes in to make it easy.'

'Good thinking. What on earth is this for?' He picked up the broken umbrella Elen had seen stranded by the storm.

'For the sea glass. We are going to hook the handle to a branch and tie sea glass to it in these little nets I found on the beach.'

'Brilliant.' Rowan admired her design.

'Let's get on with it. We have to get everything finished and this lot gone before Grandmother gets back and ruins everything. There's no time to waste!'

Chapter Eleven

The Lanterns

They worked for hours.

At last Captain Evans sat fanning himself and Captain Beaky with his cap and fondly admiring the way the vegetable patch had turned out. Nerys was still kneeling to fuss with the brightly coloured geraniums she had planted and Sally was lying back on the grass enjoying a rest with Hilary and Henrietta, her two hens.

Rowan and Elen's shell decorations tinkled in

the gentle breeze. Their umbrella hung upside down and the little nets attached to it projected jewel colours onto the grass from the sea glass. Happy little birds pecked at seeds scattered over the garden wall and newly turned-up worms. The bowls of water threw reflections of the afternoon sunlight onto the trees and against the wall. The garden looked beautiful.

Rowan whispered worriedly to Elen. 'Nothing's happening.'

'I know. Perhaps it takes a bit of time. Or perhaps the sun has to be in the right place, like in the cave.' Elen pulled at her fringe till it was almost in front of her eyes. 'How are we going to get this lot to leave before they discover our secret?'

'I'll try.' Rowan puffed his chest out and clapped his hands to get some attention. 'Thank you so much for helping us everyone. It looks brilliant. But I think you might want to … go.'

Nobody moved.

'Now,' he added.

'What, before we've had a drink for all our hard work?' Nerys looked shocked.

'I'm way too comfy to be moving yet.' Henrietta settled on Sally's chest as if to emphasise her owner's point.

'We want to admire our handiwork a little bit longer.' Captain Evans stamped his heels into the ground.

'Well, you can have one drink and then it's time to go,' Elen stated firmly. 'No arguments.'

'Yes, boss.' Captain Evans saluted then closed his eyes as if he was about to have a nap. Captain Beaky closed his eyes too.

Rowan pointed upwards. The sun was in a different position. The earth was spinning on its axis and there was no stopping it.

He and Elen rushed into the kitchen to get

some drinks. 'We'll serve these and then kick them out before the magic happens.'

'The light's fading already.' Elen was keeping an eye out of the window in case they missed anything.

'Here.' Rowan practically threw her a tray filled with drinks. Their contents sloshed everywhere but they didn't bother to wipe them up.

'Here we go.' Elen gave the drinks out. 'Drink them quickly while they are nice and chilled.'

Nerys took a small sip of hers then carried on her conversation with Sally, who also took the tiniest sip imaginable. Rowan pointed upwards. The sky was beginning to turn a very slight pink: the sunset was beginning.

'Elen, the light is going to go and there's no sign of the treasure,' he whispered. They scanned the garden desperately, hoping for some small sign to

show them where it was hidden. 'There's nothing. We need more light. What are we going to do?' Rowan was on the verge of tears.

Elen spoke to herself. 'Think, Elen, think.' She went through the lines of the poem again in her head.

Rowan's face and the sky were both turning increasingly red.

'I've got it!' she whispered, amazed she hadn't seen it before. 'The poem – the lights, the gold – it's this house. It's the lanterns themselves. They must be magic. That's why Gran is so funny about them.'

She said loudly, 'Captain Evans, as this is such a special party perhaps we should light the lanterns?'

Rowan huffed, 'But they are by the front door.'

'You got any better ideas?' Elen snapped.

'What a good idea. It's been a long time since

those lanterns have been lit. I'll do them for you now. There are some bumper-sized candles in the kitchen, I noticed.'

Elen nodded.

'It's not going to make anything magic happen.' Rowan sulked.

'You just have to believe. Both of us have to believe.' Elen crossed her fingers as the sky began to dress itself in a veil of sherbet orange. She looked back through the house as Captain Evans lit the lanterns. They flickered and glowed at the threshold as he trudged back through.

'Looks lovely with them lit. Brings back memories, I can tell you.'

'Thanks,' Elen managed to say even though her disappointment was audible.

'You're welcome. And I suppose we'd better start packing up before the old boot gets back. The boat should be on its way back by now.' He

started very slowly collecting his gardening tools. Sally cwtched both her hens and told them to sleep well and be good. Nerys seemed agitated and kept glancing at the door.

There was still no magic. Elen's brain was doing overtime trying to think of a way to make the magic work.

'Close your eyes and wish, Rowan.'

'What? That stuff's for kids.'

'It's the last chance we've got.'

'All right then.' Rowan gave the garden a final glance to make sure he hadn't missed anything then closed his eyes tight.

'On the count of three we'll open them again and something will happen.' Elen's voice sounded more convinced than she felt. 'One, two, three.'

They opened their eyes hopefully. Nothing happened.

'Try again. You really have to believe,' Elen repeated. 'The magic will only work if we both believe.'

They closed their eyes again and counted together. 'One, two, three!'

This time it felt like something was different. Nerys said, 'Elen, look.' Was this the treasure?

They opened their eyes. Elen thought she must be dreaming. She closed them again and opened them extremely slowly.

There in front of her were her mum and dad.

'Mum? Dad?'

'Elen.' Her mum squealed and ran to hug her. Her dad lifted her up in his arms and gave her the tightest embrace he'd ever given her.

'We missed you so much.' Her mum's eyes were wet. 'We decided to come back early to see you.'

'Look at all the work you've been doing for your grandmother...' Elen's dad began but was stopped by an almighty roar from within the house.

'WHO LIT THOSE LANTERNS?'

Chapter Twelve

Endings and Beginnings

Gran came storming into the back garden with a face like thunder. She was so furious she had dropped her stick and her hands were clenched into fists of rage.

'I'll have your guts for garters. I'll…'

She stopped in amazement. 'What on earth is going on here?'

Everyone stared at each other.

Elen stepped forward shakily. 'I'm sorry. It's my fault. I just wanted to make everything better and I realised that Mum and Dad didn't have much…' She stopped short of saying money, because of the other people there. 'And we wanted to find the treasure that was in the photo and you said that magical things happen here and…'

None of it seemed to make much sense when she said it out loud.

Rowan stared at his feet when Elen looked to him for help. Her grandmother still looked angry. Everyone else was still as if someone had pressed freeze on a remote control.

Elen's mum was the first to come to life. 'It's OK, Elen. It's not a secret that we don't have enough money. There's no shame in that. We've just been talking about it with Mam on the boat.'

146

'That doesn't explain who lit my lanterns.' Gran didn't look pleased about the change in the garden at all. Elen wondered if she had even noticed it.

'I'm sorry, Gran, but we wanted to make it look like it used to.' Elen gave the photo to her grandmother with trembling hands.

'We thought if we could make it beautiful and pretty and magical…' Elen's voice faltered but she found her strength and continued, 'like in the photograph … but there wasn't enough light so we had to light the lanterns.'

Gran had lost the anger, but still looked bewildered. 'That was Jack's job. Only Jack lit them.'

Elen gasped. That was why the lanterns weren't lit. Not magic at all.

Elen's mum linked her arm through Gran's. 'Mam, it's time for The Lanterns to live again. Dad would have wanted it.'

147

'I thought if I could keep everything the same…' Gran sighed. 'I've been such an old fool.'

'You haven't, Gran.' Elen took her grandmother's hand. 'You were just waiting for the magic to happen.'

'So like your mother.' Gran squeezed Elen's hand. 'I never got over Blackbeard going missing.'

'Blackbeard?' Elen shouted without meaning to.

'Your grandfather. His name was Jack but we called him Blackbeard.'

'Because of his black beard,' Elen finished, looking at the photograph. How ridiculous she'd been not to have put two and two together.

'It's my fault, Mam, I should never have left you alone for so long.' Elen's mum sounded tearful. 'We kept meaning to come back but things have been tough.'

'No, it's my fault. I should have kept in touch,' Gran replied.

'She's a stubborn old boot.' Captain Evans ventured with a cheeky wink.

'It's both our faults,' they said together, and hugged each other tight.

Elen's dad took her hand and looked at her gravely. 'You can say no to this, Elen. It's just a suggestion and it might not work out and we won't give it a go if you don't want to...'

'It's all right, Dad. What is it?' Elen felt as if she had grown up about five years since she'd come to the island.

'We've had difficulty making ends meet, as you know, after I lost my job.' He cleared his throat. 'But we've chatted to your grandmother and the products she makes here are remarkable, so we thought perhaps we could move here and help her to make them and sell them. As a family-run business.'

'So I'd have to move to the island?' Elen could hardly believe her ears.

'Yes,' her mum said. 'I know it would be a huge change and you'd have to go to a new school … and you can say no if you want to.'

Everyone waited with baited breath.

'Of course I want to move here!' Elen whooped loudly. 'Who wouldn't want to live on the most brilliant island in the world!'

They all cheered and startled the hens into a flurry of squawking. Captain Beaky waddled around in circles then jumped up into the air beating his wings rapidly.

The clock in the hall struck loudly much to Elen's grandmother's astonishment. 'That's the first time that clock has worked since your grandfather was lost!'

Captain Evans stepped forward. 'Time for a new beginning perhaps?'

'I'll drink to that!' Sally exclaimed happily.

'Let's make this a proper party and get some music going.' Nerys took out a tin whistle from her bag and started to play.

'Madam. If I may?' Captain Evans held his hand out to Elen's grandmother.

She looked thoughtful for a second then straightened up and took his hand. She cried as they began to dance, but she was smiling too.

Sally picked up Hilary and Henrietta and began to whirl with them tucked safely in the crooks of her arms.

Elen's mum and dad laughed then joined in spinning and swirling around the garden. Elen had never seen them so happy. She looked at Rowan.

Rowan was fussing over his puffin. 'I think this will be our last night together, Captain Beaky. You're well enough to be set free tomorrow,' Rowan choked.

'I'm sure he'll fly back for a visit.' Elen smiled gently at Rowan. 'You are going to be lifelong friends.'

She looked at him apologetically. 'There's no treasure and there's no magic,' she said sadly.

He turned. 'Are you kidding? This is the magic. You having all your family together is the gold, isn't it?' He looked enviously at them then

152

grinned at Elen. 'But no way am I dancing, so don't even ask.'

Elen pushed her fringe out of her eyes and looked at the garden's happy gathering, realising that Rowan was right. This was the treasure and, as the stars started to sprinkle the sky in glittering patterns, she grabbed hold of Rowan's arm and giggled happily.

'Oh yes you are!'

The Dragonfly series from *Firefly*

Dragonfly

Dragon Gold
Shoo Rayner – £5.99

Dragon White
Shoo Rayner – £5.99

Dragon Red
Shoo Rayner – £5.99

Arthur and Me
Sarah Todd Taylor – £4.99

Dottie Blanket and the Hilltop
Wendy Meddour – £4.99

Elen's Island
Eloise Williams – £5.99

**Grace-Ella,
Spells for Beginners**
Sharon Marie Jones – £5.99

**Mr Mahli's Shed and a
Ghost named Dylan**
Laura Sheldon – £5.99

Pete and the Five-a-Side Vampires
Malachy Doyle – £4.99

Steve's Dreams: Steve and the Sabretooth Tiger
Dan Anthony – £4.99

Steve and the Singing Pirates
Dan Anthony – £5.99

Thimble Monkey Superstar
Jon Blake – £5.99

Dragonfly books are funny, scary, fantastical and exciting.

www.fireflypress.co.uk/dragonfly